"Did you see it?" a young gi
past Gabe in the café. "The nativ
back, sitting right in the center of
there's another new piece."

"Is it the baby, Jesus?" the girl's mother asked hopefully as she bent down toward her daughter.

The child shook her head.

"Well, what is it, Annabelle?"

"An angel," she whispered.

The woman stood up straight and maneuvered, trying to glance out the window, but the café didn't lend itself well to a view of Town Square.

"What on earth are you looking at, Mable?" a woman in a large purple hat asked, bending down and pulling back the curtain.

"Annabelle said the nativity is back."

The café quieted and it seemed all ears had turned to her.

"It's been four years," a man, Gabe couldn't see, called out. "You'd think there would at least be a baby in that manger."

"I think it's sweet. After all, aren't we all waiting for Jesus?" Mable placed a hand on her daughter's shoulder.

Little Annabelle looked over at Gabe and her eyes widened, sparkling with a gleam, and she smiled. She tugged on her mother's skirt.

"Well, it certainly has brought some hope back to Thistleberry. It seems right fitting that it's an angel."

Also by

KELLI ANN MORGAN

THE RANCHER
REDBOURNE SERIES BOOK ONE

THE BOUNTY HUNTER
REDBOURNE SERIES BOOK TWO

THE BLACKSMITH
REDBOURNE SERIES BOOK THREE

THE IRON HORSEMAN
REDBOURNE SERIES BOOK FOUR

THE OUTRIDER
REDBOURNE SERIES BOOK FIVE

THE WRANGLER
REDBOURNE SERIES BOOK SIX

THE LUMBERJACK
REDBOURNE SERIES BOOK SEVEN

THE LAWMAN
REDBOURNE SERIES BOOK EIGHT

JONAH
DEARDON MINI-SERIES BOOK ONE

LUCAS
DEARDON MINI-SERIES BOOK TWO

NOAH
DEARDON MINI-SERIES BOOK THREE

Available from INSPIRE BOOKS

An Angel in Thistleberry

DEARDON FAMILY REUNION

KELLI ANN
MORGAN

Inspire Books
A Division of Inspire Creative Services
937 West 1350 North, Clinton, Utah 84015, USA

While some of the events described and some of the characters depicted in this book may be loosely based on actual historical events and real historical figures, this book is a work of fiction. Other names, characters, places, and incidents either are the product of the author's imagination or are used factitiously, and any resemblance to actual persons, living or dead, business establishments, events, or locales is entirely coincidental. The publisher does not have any control over and does not assume any responsibility for author or third-party websites or their content.

AN ANGEL IN THISTLEBERRY

An Inspire Book published by arrangement with the author

Second Inspire Books paperback edition December 2018

Cover Design by Kelli Ann Morgan at Inspire Creative Services

ISBN-13: 978-1-939049-52-0
ISBN-10: 1939049520

Printed in the United States of America

PRAISE FOR THE NOVELS OF AMAZON BESTSELLING AUTHOR

KELLI ANN MORGAN

"Morgan really knows how to weave a tale."

—*CiCi J* on HOLDEN'S HEART

"The Redbourne men are the most amazing characters in the American west!"

—*Lesia Chambliss* on THE IRON HORSEMAN

"…just when you think things are starting to settle down, a whole new twist begins!"

—*Kathy Hathaway* on THE WRANGLER

"Excellent, well-written plot that kept me reading past bedtime."

—*Kindle Customer* on THE WRANGLER

"...starts off with a bang that will keep you in stitches..."

—*Cyn* on THE RANCHER

"…stayed up half the night and I am half dead this morning, but oh so worth it."

—*The eBook Investigator* on THE RANCHER

"...a book to read any day of the week or season. It had just the right balance of romance and intrigue."

—*Linda M.* on JONAH

"A must read for anyone who enjoys westerns with adventure, romance, and humor."

—*Amazon Customer* on THE BOUNTY HUNTER

"A phenomenal read...a must have for any library."

—*Kindle Customer* on THE OUTRIDER

"...flying through, but I truly don't want them to end!!!"

—*Deborah Roth* on THE BLACKSMITH

To all of my wonderful fans who really
wanted to see Gabe's story stand on its own…

An Angel in Thistleberry

DEARDON FAMILY REUNION

CHAPTER ONE

Whisper Ridge Ranch, Thistleberry, Montana, November 1883

Snow fell.

The absence of his family enshrouded Gabriel Deardon with a hefty weight. His dreams had left him restless and with a feeling of emptiness. He ripped the quilt from atop of him and sprung out of his bed as quickly as his old bones would allow.

There was work to be done.

His checkered shirt draped over the high-backed chair in his room. He strung his arms through the sleeves, pulled on his worn boots and old, faded hat, then gingerly made his way out into the living area and to the front door. He lifted his heavy wool-lined coat from the rack and donned it as he treaded out toward the barn, pulling the collar up around his ears.

The barn door slid open easily now that his nephews had seen to oiling the hinges, and he closed himself inside, rubbing his hands together and blowing his warm breath into them. Gloves would be no use for what he needed to do. He lit the lantern, hanging on a hook just to the side of him.

In the far corner of the barn, in a stall scarcely large enough to contain a pony, Gabe glanced over his shoulder before setting down his lamp and moving a few small boxes and barrels aside to allow him access to the discarded worktable that sat up against the wall. He pulled back the saddle blanket that had been thrown over several mid-sized crates he'd hidden there.

It would only be an hour or so before the others would arise and the daily chores on the ranch would begin. He bent down to lift the first box and froze when an excruciating spasm blazed the trail from his hip to his shoulder.

"Blast it all!" he cursed, sucking air into his lungs. His hand shot to his back, and he forced himself into a standing position once again. After a few moments, he bent his creaking knees and crouched down enough that he was able to retrieve his intended crate, then heaved it up onto the countertop with some effort. He reached in and pulled out a large cut of wood and several tools.

His lower back hurt and his movements were stiff, but he had more important things on his mind than how his body ached, and his bones creaked.

There was no time to waste.

Deardon Ranch, Oregon

"The offer is a very good one," Jonah Deardon spoke quietly as he sat at the kitchen table, his hands folded together and resting against his forehead.

His wife, Emma, slid onto the bench next to him, running her hand along the curve of his back before placing an open envelope down in front of him. "This came today."

He glanced down at the letter, then turned to look at her.

She smiled, sliding her hand down the length of his arm until it rested in the curve of his elbow. She leaned down, resting her chin on his shoulder.

Jonah picked up the correspondence to inspect it more closely.

The postmark read, *Thistleberry, Montana.*

"More good news," he said with a snort, unable to keep the sarcasm from his voice.

"Lucy has invited us to come stay at Whisper Ridge for the holidays. She writes that the property next to the ranch will be sold at auction just after Thanksgiving."

Jonah leaned his head down to rest against Emma's.

She missed their children. He sensed it even more now that the holidays were approaching. With work growing more scarce in their little Oregon town, many families had moved away and opportunities for courtship or even developing friendships were increasingly difficult to find. Grown now, with wills of their own, the twins and Owen had left home just over a year ago to visit family at Whisper Ridge in Thistleberry, Montana, and had decided to stay. Only their youngest, August, remained at home.

"Have I told you today just how much I love you?" Jonah asked as he bent down and kissed his wife on the tip of her nose.

"Yes," she replied with a smile that still melted his heart, "but I never tire of hearing it," she finished, raising her head enough he could look into her beautiful face.

"I love you, Emma Deardon."

"And I you."

He bent down and placed a light kiss on her lips, enjoying their sweet taste.

With a deep breath, Jonah picked up the letter and pulled it from the envelope. He scanned the contents and ground his teeth together. The property had everything they had been waiting for, but…

"What is it that's stopping you, Jonah? Are you worried about seeing your father?" Emma interrupted his thoughts.

How did she always know what he was thinking?

"Spending the holidays with Gabe Deardon has never been pleasant. I'm not sure I want to expose our children to such a Scrooge on a more permanent basis."

It's a little late for that, Deardon, he thought the moment the words left his mouth.

Emma smiled and placed her hands over Jonah's. "If you'll remember, darling, even Ebenezer Scrooge had a change of heart."

Truth was, Jonah missed being with his family—his brothers, his children. Some of the best times he'd had over the years had been with his cousins and their families. It was time to move on. He knew it, but the thought of living next to his father sent a pit to his stomach that he couldn't dispel.

"Not my father. He's as ornery as they come." Jonah pushed his seat away from the table and walked to the edge of the fireplace where Emma had already begun collecting pinecones for a Christmas mantel piece.

"Jonah," Emma said knowingly, joining him at the hearth,

"it's time. We'll never get another offer like the one Mr. MacPherson has proposed."

He wrapped his arm around his wife's shoulders and leaned down to kiss the top of her head.

"I know." He placed the letter behind the small collection of pinecones. "I know."

CHAPTER TWO

Thistleberry, Montana

"Did you see it?" a young girl exclaimed as she skipped past Gabe in the café. "The nativity," she said excitedly, "it's back, sitting right in the center of Town Square. And mother, there's another new piece."

"Is it the baby, Jesus?" the girl's mother asked hopefully as she bent down toward her daughter.

The child shook her head.

"Well, what is it, Annabelle?"

"An angel," she whispered.

The woman stood up straight and maneuvered, trying to glance out the window, but the café didn't lend itself well to a view of Town Square.

"What on earth are you looking at, Mable?" a woman in a large purple hat asked, bending down and pulling back the curtain.

"Annabelle said the nativity is back."

The café quieted and it seemed all ears had turned to her.

"It's been four years," a man Gabe couldn't see called out. "You'd think there would at least be a baby in that manger."

"I think it's sweet." Mable placed a hand on her daughter's shoulder. "After all, aren't we all waiting for Jesus?"

Little Annabelle looked over at Gabe who raised a brow, and her eyes widened, sparkling with a gleam. She smiled, then tugged on her mother's skirt.

"Well, it certainly has brought some hope back to Thistleberry. It seems right fitting that it's an angel." The woman in the purple hat stood up straight and nodded.

"Do you think it was Father Christmas?" The waitress' shrill voice carried from the table behind Gabe.

The little girl tugged again on her mother's skirt.

"Certainly, you don't believe in such nonsense, Cornelia Wilson?" another young woman called out with a giggle.

"Of course, I do," Cornelia retorted. "How else would that bag of foodstuffs have just appeared on the Doherty's porch when they'd just eaten their last loaf of old, dried out, and crumbly bread?"

"Or how did a carved bedframe and down-filled mattress show up on the Jensen's doorstep when they moved into town with nary a chair to sit in?" The girl's mother chimed in.

Gabe smiled despite himself.

"I see your point."

"Speaking of those in need, did you hear?" Cornelia started and the others quieted to listen as the young mother moved past Gabe to join in their conversation.

Annabelle stopped in front of his table and looked up at him discerningly. She tilted her head from one side to the other, then she raised her elbow up to rest on his table and leaned in.

"Are you," she asked with a voice barely above a whisper, "Father Christmas?"

Gabe nearly choked on the sip of apple cider he'd just taken.

The girl giggled as he mopped up the drink from his beard. He set down his napkin and winked at the child, placing a single finger over his lips.

Her eyes grew wide, and a knowing smile spread across her features. She nodded. Then, she rounded the table, walked up to him, and stood as tall as she could on her tiptoes. He leaned down, expecting her to whisper a secret, but she placed a light kiss on his cheek.

"Thank you," she whispered and quickly joined her mother, who was already in deep conversation with the other ladies.

Gabe's insides warmed his outsides. Annabelle reminded him of his own little granddaughter, Sophia, who'd been named after his mother. From the day she'd been born, they'd had a special bond that had incited him to start something special.

"Several of the men lost their jobs at the mill," Cornelia was saying as he returned his attention to the chatter. "Dear Mr. Collins was among them. His poor wife. I don't know what they'll do. I guess there just isn't much work for them during the winter months."

Gabe took another sip at his hot apple cider, his ears perked to the conversation behind him.

"They really depended on the work," she continued, "and without the money, they're going to lose their house. Mr. Crumpett at the bank owns the deed and, well, you know him. They'll be thrown out in the cold with all seven of their children. And just before Christmas." The town busybody tsked loudly.

Shame, Gabe thought.

Mr. Collins was like that good kindly fellow with his grump of an employer in the Christmas book Lucy had given him to read.

What was his name? Gabe squinted as if the action would increase his memory, with no such luck.

"Ah, it'll come to me," he dismissed quietly.

"I'm sorry, Mr. Deardon, did you need something?" Cornelia asked, popping her head around the table.

Thistleberry had always been a close-knit community, but Gabe had often chosen to keep his distance from the townsfolk here—especially from women like Cornelia, who gossiped as much as the day was long. However, her heart seemed to be in the right place, and he'd found a use for her gossip—especially at Christmastime—and so he smiled to himself as he shook his head, raised his cup toward the woman, then took another sip of his drink.

The wind blustered outside and a bare branch with a single leaf that seemed to be clinging on for life, scratched eerily against the windowpane. A cold chill trickled down his arms and he shook it off, delaying his departure another moment as he tipped the bottom of his mug trying to extract every last drop of the deliciously warm concoction.

Resigned to the inevitable, he pulled some money from his pocket and slid it beneath the base of the cup. He slipped on the thick coat with woolen interior, and grabbed his hat from the rack at the edge of his table. He tipped the brim at Lyla, the owner of the place, as he braced himself for the cold weather.

"Oh, Dad, there you are," Lucy, his daughter-in-law, said as she balanced a couple of boxes in her arms.

"Here," he said, reaching out, "let me take some of those."

They walked over to the livery where they'd stowed the wagon.

"Did you get what you came for?" Lucy asked with a twinkle in her eye.

"Yes, ma'am. Just need to make one quick stop on the way home." He loaded the boxes into the back of the buckboard, then turned back to Lucy and clapped his hands together, rubbing them against the cold. "Ready?'

"You seem a little…giddy." Lucy scrunched her eyes and then raised one brow. "What are you up to Gabe Deardon?"

He dropped the smile from his face and donned a scowl. "Me? Giddy? Absurd."

"Back to one-word answers. That's more like the Gabe I know." She stepped up onto her tiptoes and placed a kiss on his cheek.

Pleased, heat flooded his face.

He cleared his throat.

"Storm's coming in. We'd better be on our way." Gabe held out his hand and helped Lucy up into the wagon.

It didn't take long for them to reach the mill. He climbed down, his cracking knees evoking a grunt from him as he reached the ground, but he couldn't help the little jaunt that had worked its way into his stride. He had to consciously slow his step to avoid any further suspicion.

A little bell rang as he opened the front door into the mill office, and the moment he saw Ethel Fawcett, he froze. An awkward smile tried to break onto his face, but his breath caught in his chest, and he spun back around and placed his hand on the wooden handle to leave.

"Did you need something, Mr. Deardon?" Ethel asked in a voice that spilled like warm butter down his shoulders.

He dropped his head, turned back to face her, and removed his hat.

"Uh, yes, ma'am," he said, "I'm looking for your son. Is Myron here?"

"He is," she confirmed. "He's just out in the yard." She

pointed to the back door that led out to the barn-like structure where men were working the saws. "Is there something I might do for you?" She looked up at him with eyes that sparkled in the light.

"I just need a word with him, ma'am."

"Oh," she said, and Gabe thought he detected a note of disappointment in her voice.

Maybe he'd just imagined it.

"All right, then," she said with a nod. "You can head on out."

"If you'll excuse me." Gabe placed his hat back on his head and tapped the brim.

"I must say, Mr. Deardon," she called before he could get out the door, "that beard is coming along quite handsomely."

Heat flooded his neck and he reached up self-consciously to stroke the lengthening whiskers. He winked at her brazenly, then strode out into the back without a second glance behind him.

Once outside, Gabe released a long breath. How did that woman affect him so? Wasn't he a little too old to let a woman get under his skin?

Myron, the owner of the mill, looked up from one of the boards he was cutting. As soon as the wood had made its way over the saw blade, the man turned it off, then wiped his hands on his apron and jutted his hand out to shake Gabe's.

"I'm glad you stopped by, Deardon. It saves me a trip out to your place. I'm afraid your lumber order has been delayed."

"What do you mean my lumber has been...delayed," Gabe grumped at the man.

He was running out of time. That wood was necessary to complete the majority of his special projects, and he'd counted on having it here this week. With the addition of today's discovery about the Collins family, he would need even more.

"An emergency order came in from Middleton and I'm a little shorthanded right now."

"Shorthanded indeed. Word has it that you just laid off several of your men. Holidays are coming. A lot of folks are going to have a real hard time of it."

Myron's face flushed and Gabe immediately regretted his judgement. Old habits were hard to break—even after years of trying.

"Humville?" Gabe didn't much care for Middleton's mayor.

The mill owner nodded.

"Well, I've got a large order of my own to place in addition to the one I'm still expecting. Half of it doesn't even need to be cut. I can do that myself."

"How large an order?" Myron asked, scratching his chin.

"Big enough it will make Old Humville's order look like beans." He made sure to catch the man's eyes. "And I'm willing to pay handsomely—if you can have it delivered out to Whisper Ridge no less than two weeks before Christmas.

"Why that's only a couple weeks from now."

He handed the mill owner a scrap of paper with his offer written on it.

Myron whistled softly as he looked down at the number.

Gabe hadn't used any of his inheritance in more than thirty years—not since his wife had left him with four small boys to raise on his own. At least that was up until a few years ago after his only granddaughter was born.

Little Sophia had affected him in ways that he couldn't explain. She'd inspired him to be a better man and to do something meaningful with the rest of whatever life he had left and somehow make up for his past wrongs.

Now was as good a time as any to use that money.

"As generous as this is, Mr. Deardon, how am I supposed to get an order like that fulfilled in that time?"

Gabe didn't say anything, but stared at the man and waited.

"I guess I could hire Mr. Collins back—temporarily mind you," he noted with a raised finger. "And maybe some of the others."

There it is.

"Cratchit!" Gabe yelled out.

"I'm sorry." Myron looked at him as if he'd gone mad.

"Bob Cratchit." Gabe laughed remembering the name of the character in that book who'd reminded him of Mr. Collins.

Good man.

"Who?"

Gabe cleared his throat and returned a stern expression to his face. "Never you mind. Just get me that lumber."

CHAPTER THREE

December

As Noah Deardon pulled through the gates of the Whisper Ridge Ranch with his little family, it took everything he had to stop himself from slapping the reins of the wagon team to incite them to move faster over the compressed snow path. It had been a long time since he'd seen his brothers. Christmas had been nothing more than an inconvenience in the Deardon household when he was young, but over the last few years he'd grown to love the holiday. Kate, his wife, loved Christmas and took every opportunity to make it a special time full of love and laughter.

"Does Uncle Lucas have any children for us to play with?" Easton, Noah's oldest son of twelve, asked as they came to a stop in front of the homestead.

Noah placed a hand on his son's shoulder and squeezed. "Not your age, I'm afraid, but we do have a lot of extended family here and I'm sure you will make friends with all your cousins in no time," he reassured the boy.

Lucas and Lucy had struggled with having children up until a few years ago when little Sophia had come along.

He held up a hand for Kate, and helped her down from the cold wagon seat, then placed her lightly on the ground with a quick kiss. With a deep breath, Noah stepped up to the front door, ready to burst in, but before he could grasp the handle, it squeaked open and a little girl with a headful of bouncy curls looked up at them with wide eyes.

"Hello," she said with a smile that looked just like her father's. "Who are you?"

"Hello, Sophia," Noah said, dropping down to a knee in front of her.

"How do you know my name?" she asked in a small voice, her eyes wide and twinkling with wonder.

"Well, I…" he wasn't sure how to answer her.

"It's Uncle Noah, dear. Daddy's brother," Lucy Deardon said as she placed her arm on the little girl's shoulders and gently nudged her forward.

Sophia gasped with delight and jumped forward unexpectedly with a hug around his neck. "I'm so glad you're here!" she squealed, holding him tighter than he would have expected.

Noah stood up, his arms wrapped around her, basking in the attentions of his little four-year-old niece. Girls were hard to come by in his family, but when they arrived, they were always something special.

When she pulled back to look at his face, she still beamed at him. "It's a pleasure to make your acquaintance," she said with a slight nod of her head. Then, she looked down at his boys who still stood on the steps.

Noah set her down on the ground with an amused grin.

"That means you must be…" she looked up at the air, as if trying to remember, "Easton, Gavin, Quinn, and Ian," she said the last as she pointed up at the toddler in Kate's arms.

Each of the boys' eyes lit up as she said their names.

Kate giggled.

"Come on," she said, grabbing Gavin by the hand and dragging him into the house. "We have to let Papa know that you're here."

Easton looked up at his father for approval.

Noah nodded and the boys happily followed Sophia inside.

"She is beautiful, Lucy," Kate said, wrapping her arms around her sister-in-law.

"She's been practicing everyone's names for days," Lucy said with a laugh, reaching out to hug Noah as well. "Where are my manners? Come in. Come in. Lucas will be so glad to see you. We weren't expecting you until early next week, so give me a minute and I'll just get your room fixed up."

Noah stepped inside and placed a large travelling case on the floor next to the door.

"Can I help?" Kate asked, switching baby Ian to her other hip.

Lucy nodded and grasped his wife by the hand, then turned back to look at Noah. "I think the men are all out in the barn. There is plenty of room for your wagon and stalls for the horses. Jake will help you see to them." With that, she, like her daughter, pulled Kate into the house and disappeared.

Noah breathed out a laugh and turned back to take care of the wagon.

When Lucy had first contacted them about coming to Whisper Ridge for the holidays, Noah had been reluctant. After his mother had left them to sing on a big city stage when he was but nine years old, it had only been him, his three brothers, and their father—who had decided that Christmas was just another working day—and happy memories during the holiday season at that time were hard to come by.

Sentimentality had not been a priority in their home, and while he and his brothers had been close, they'd not experienced the same type of family life they'd seen when they visited their cousins at Redbourne Ranch in Stone Creek, Kansas. Besides, he'd reasoned, Thistleberry was a long way from Laramie and would be an arduous journey with his little ones—especially since the rail line had not yet been completed between the two places.

However, being married to Kate and starting a family of their own had changed him. And what he'd once believed to be simply an unachievable ideal, only experienced by others, had grown into a reality he and his wife had created for their own children. When he'd finally realized just how much he'd missed his brothers…and his dad—though that was the hardest to admit, he'd sent a telegram back to Lucy with a resounding yes.

Gabe Deardon was a stubborn man, and none of his sons had ever seen eye to eye with their father, but Noah felt life was too short to allow misunderstandings and petty differences to get in the way of family. Besides, his father had been at Whisper Ridge now for several years, and he hoped that in that time, the man would have taken the opportunity to reconnect with his own brothers and with Lucas, and that maybe he'd been able to find a way to make peace with his past.

Still, Noah couldn't help his desire to have his father be proud of him and all he'd accomplished.

As he stepped off the front porch, he looked over to the barn, where he saw Lucas already running across the snow toward him. A few strides closed the distance between them, and he pulled his not-so-little brother into a fierce hug. Noah clenched his jaw, refusing to allow the tears welling up in his eyes to escape down his face. He just held on. It had been so long.

"I didn't think you were going to be here until next week," Lucas finally said once they pulled apart. "Where are Kate and the kids?"

"The boys are with that little sweetheart of yours. Does that girl just have you wrapped around her little finger? She is a doll."

Lucas laughed. "Sounds like she's already worked her charms on you. I know she's got Dad right where she wants him."

Noah stared at Lucas. "No," he said, disbelievingly.

"Sure does." His brother nodded. "Dad is like a different man when that little girl is around."

"This I've got to see."

"You will."

CHAPTER FOUR

The sound of several small voices outside the door alerted Gabe to his granddaughter's presence.

"It's here! It's here!" The excited squeals of the little girl had him on his feet in moments, and he opened the door.

"What's here?" he asked.

Sophia took his hand and dragged him all through the house until they reached the front door where Lucy stood, watching, her hand resting at her chest.

As he made his way to the entrance and stood over the threshold, he glanced out into the yard and was greeted by a sight he hadn't thought he would ever see again. His boys—all but Henry, God rest his soul, inspected the new handcrafted sleigh his sister's kid, Ethan, had made and shipped to him from Kansas.

His emotions ran high. He clenched his jaw and ground his teeth to help quell the emotion that threatened to surface. He opened his mouth to call out, but fear overtook him, and he took two steps backward into the living room away from the door.

How could he face them?

Lucy glanced back over her shoulder. "Gabe. Can you believe it? They're here. All together. Finally."

"Come on, Granddad. What are you waiting for?" Sophia tugged on him, but he stood his ground.

"Nobody asked them to come," he said gruffly as he pulled his hand from the little girl's steady grip, then dropped down as far as his knees would allow and placed a light kiss on the tip of the child's small nose. His heart flooded with mixed emotions as she stared at him questioningly. "Maybe later," he added.

"Gabe," Lucy tried to stop him as he strode to the kitchen, "your sleigh is here," she called after him. "Didn't you see it?"

He ignored her. Of course, he'd seen it, but he hadn't been prepared to see his boys as they eyed and felt the sleigh in child-like wonder, thinking of all the memories he'd deprived them of growing up because of his stupid pride. Years of Christmases had been ruined with grief and bitterness.

Gabe threw open the back door and headed out to the barn. He hadn't been a good father, hadn't been there for them when they'd needed him most, and he didn't blame any of them for the resentment they felt for him. Regret for the years his anger had stolen from them had been his constant companion of late, but nothing could make up for lost time.

Coming to Whisper Ridge had allowed him the opportunity to repair much of his relationship with Lucas over the last few years, but the boy had been the youngest—barely seven—when their mother had left, and his recollection of that time was limited. Life now was very different. He was different.

He wiped a rogue tear from the corner of his eye and threw back the blanket hiding his little treasures. Most of them had been completed, but there were several that still needed sanding and a little paint.

"Why, Gabe Deardon, if I didn't know any better I would say you are hiding."

He whipped around to see his daughter-in-law, Emma, standing in the doorway, her hands tucked into a blue fur muff. A grin spread across her face as she made her way toward him.

"It's good to see you," she said, leaning down and placing a kiss on his cheek. "Lucy said I'd probably find you out here. I hope you don't mind."

Gabe didn't know what to say, so he just picked up the piece of wood he'd been carving and started sanding the edges. The last time he'd seen Emma, he'd just had words with Jonah and had left things on uncertain terms when he moved to Montana.

"We did it," she said as she sat down on the stool next to him. "We bought the MacPherson place."

Gabe shot her a surprised look, then returned his focus to his work, but couldn't help the smile that tugged on the corners of his mouth.

"And the ranch?" he finally choked out.

"Sold it." Emma placed the muff on the top of the worktable and placed a hand on Gabe's shoulder. "I suppose that means we will be seeing a lot more of each other."

He thought about saying something sarcastic, but couldn't force the words.

"I'd like that," he said simply.

"Did Ethan really make that sleigh?" Kate asked as she appeared at the back of the barn.

"Isn't it beautiful?" Lucy asked, joining them and pulling the large door closed behind her. "I still can't believe you had it shipped in, Gabe. I'm sure Mr. Gibbons would have been willing to make something for you. Unless…"

The town's blacksmith was handy enough in his trade, but the type of intricate design work and sturdy durability he'd wanted could only come from the hands of his talented nephew, Ethan Redbourne.

"Unless what?" he asked with a raised brow.

All three women gathered in close around him.

"Unless you didn't want everyone in town to know that sleigh belongs to you."

"What are you talking about?" He looked down at the train in his hands and quickly shoved it back into the box and dusted off his hands. "I think you've all gone mad."

He didn't fluster easily, but having all three of his daughters-in-law closing in on him, he'd begun to feel cornered.

Lucy pulled the blanket off of the rocking horse he'd just finished last night.

"Ah," the women collectively gasped.

"Oh, Dad, it's stunning."

"So," Gabe said with a shrug, "I'm making myself useful. What is it you think you know?"

"I think we're looking at Thistleberry's own Father Christmas," Lucy said happily.

"That's ridiculous," he challenged, but knew there wasn't much use denying it.

He'd been caught.

The women each placed their hands on their hips, grins spread across their faces.

"How can we help?"

Gabe glanced to the doorway where Ethel Fawcett had poked her head in. She slipped inside, a deep red mantle draped over her arm. He slid back the stool and jumped to his feet, his knees cracking at the effort.

"Mrs. Fawcett?" he said, self-consciously slicking his white hair down with his hand.

"We've known each other a long while now, Gabriel Deardon. Don't you think it's about time you called me Ethel?"

Gabe flitted a glance at each of his daughters-in-law and bowed his head before looking back at the woman—striking in her deep green dress. "Yes, ma'am, I reckon so, but how—?" He was still a little confused as to how all of these women had any idea what he'd been up to.

"I've always had a sense about you." She winked and Gabe thought his heart might bust the buttons on the front of his shirt.

"What can I do for you…Ethel?"

She held up the drape from her arm—a crimson cloak that boasted finished brown, fur-lined cuffs, collar, and hemline. It looked like something out of a Father Christmas storybook.

"It's for you," Ethel said. "Lucy and the girls over at Happenstance worked hard to make the material from their finest wool and I, well I added a few touches of my own."

He took a step toward her, but didn't dare reach out for it. He was sure the color heating his face matched the hue of the coat Mrs. Fawcett held out to him. He couldn't help the smile that cracked his features as all four women beamed at him.

No one was supposed to find out about the things he'd been doing for folks around town the last couple of years. Raine, the town sheriff and his sister's oldest kid, was the only one who knew what he'd been up to. And that was only because he'd caught Gabe trying to unload a huge bedframe and mattress by himself from a wagon in the middle of the night. He'd been helping him in secret ever since, but Gabe had been extra careful after that not to call any attention to himself. It was always anonymous, a mystery, and he liked it that way.

"What am I supposed to do now?" he asked, shaking his head.

He couldn't just stop. People needed him, maybe for the first time in a long time. Even though they didn't know it was him.

"Just continue to be the angel we all know you to be."

"We just want you to keep warm while doing it," Lucy said.

He didn't move.

"Well, go ahead. Try it on." Ethel held it out for him.

This was silly. And Gabe Deardon was not a silly man, so why did he want to try it on?

"Oh, for heaven's sake, Dad." Lucy got behind Ethel and nudged her closer to Gabe.

His heartbeat quickened as the woman held open the cloak and waited.

As he slipped one arm through the coat, the weight of it enveloped him in warmth. He quickly donned the rest of it, wrapping it eagerly around his front.

"I'm afraid I don't have the right belly for it." He patted his lean stomach.

The women laughed.

"You look wonderful, Gabe," Emma beamed at him.

"Very handsome," Kate confirmed.

"A right Father Christmas," Lucy added.

He turned away from them, refusing to allow his emotions to get the better of him. It wasn't long before he was encircled in the encouraging and loving embraces of the women who meant the most to him in this world—minus one little angel who couldn't know his secret. At least not yet.

"Thank you," he whispered. "And you really want to help?"

Each of them nodded eagerly.

"Well then," he said with a slight crack in his voice and cleared his throat. "Let's get to work."

CHAPTER FIVE

"I understand the need for a sleigh in a Montana winter, but isn't this a little extravagant for Dad?" Jonah asked as he admired the hand-crafted embellishments that lined the edges of the large red contraption.

Lucas looked up at his oldest brother, then over at Noah, who had climbed up into the front seat of the sleigh. It was so good to have them here at Whisper Ridge for the holidays and he wished they would stay forever. He'd missed them.

"It's so intricate and detailed," Jonah said as he worked his way to the front. "I haven't seen this kind of craftmanship since…" His voice trailed and he looked back and forth between his brothers, one brow raised and a knowing smile on his lips.

"Aunt Leah," they all said in unison.

They laughed.

"That's the only explanation. Right? That Ethan made this sleigh?" Jonah asked.

"Do you remember the time when we all forgot it was Christmas day until old Mrs. Perkins felt sorry for us that we didn't have a mother and dropped by with some of her homemade holiday confections?" Noah laughed as he climbed into the back section of the sleigh and lifted the lid to a little storage compartment at the rear.

"Or the time that Mrs. Blake tried to 'brighten' up the place with pine boughs and holly and Dad ripped them off the wall and the fireplace mantle, then we spent half the morning cleaning up the needles and squished berries from the floorboards." Jonah shook his head, leaning down to inspect the thick, ornately decorated leather straps dangling from the front seat. "I think Tag must have helped," he mused, holding up the reins.

Their cousin, Tag Redbourne, was every bit as talented with hide as his brother was with metal.

Lucas nodded.

"What about the time that Henry tried to strap sticks to the new pony's head like one of Santa's reindeer from that book Aunt Leah sent us and the colt kicked back and broke the lantern and started a hay bale on fire?" Noah mused as he leaned against the sleigh, resting his folded arms on the edge.

The thought of their oldest brother brought a sense of solemnity to otherwise jovial banter. They'd lost Henry a little over thirteen years ago, but his memory lingered with each of them every day.

They looked a sad lot.

Henry would be disappointed that they allowed his memory to be sad.

"No, the best yet, was when Henry tried to plunk out the tune for 'We Wish You a Merry Christmas' on the old piano and Dad very calmly pushed it out into the yard and chopped it into firewood," Lucas said, recounting his first real Christmas memory. "I still can't believe he banned music in the house." He looked up at Jonah whose face had drained of color, his mouth gaping.

"You were so young then. I didn't know you remembered that," he said with a hint of pity in his voice.

"What?" Lucas asked, surprised by his brothers' reactions. "Don't you?"

"Of course, but I was much older than you."

"I hardly call five years 'much older'."

"Six."

"Six then. I don't remember much before Mother left, but there are some things I can't seem to forget." He looked from Jonah to Noah and back again, their brows scrunched together and Jonah's jaw flexing. He'd seen that look before and it was usually followed by a confrontation with their father.

"It was a long time ago," Lucas dismissed as he reached for the large potato sack drape they had pulled from the sleigh. "Henry would have been the first to tell us that we need to find the good in things instead of focusing on the bad or the things we can't change. Besides, Dad is a different man now." He tossed one side of the cloth up and over the seats while Noah grabbed ahold of the other side and together they covered their father's unlikely purchase.

Jonah snorted as he reached down for his bags.

"Emma had been missing our boys something fierce," he said, obviously attempting to change the subject. "Are they around?"

"I think the twins are still out with Uncle Hank, Raine, and Andrew helping clear out the rest of the MacPherson place for the new owners next door."

It wasn't like Mr. MacPherson to be so secretive, but he hadn't let slip the name of the new owner. Claimed they'd preferred to keep it a secret for now. To be discreet.

"I guess it really shouldn't matter," Lucas said, stepping down from the sleigh and securing one of the ropes. "Just seems odd that they would make a point not to let folks know their names."

"Maybe it's someone famous," Noah chimed in. "Or wanted."

"It would just be nice to know something about them."

Jonah cleared his throat.

"You're…uh…looking at them. Him," he corrected with a grin as he sauntered toward the house.

It took a moment for his words to register correctly.

"Wait. What?" Lucas tied the tarp strings around the metal cleat that had been placed in the siding just below the driver's seat, then hustled into the house behind his brother, Noah on his heels.

They passed through the kitchen and into the living room where they were greeted by a moment of chaos as everyone there were hugging everyone else. Jonah kissed his wife smack dab on the mouth, then turned to face them, his arm still around Emma's waist as he beamed at the surprise.

"Mother?" multiple voices exclaimed all at once coming from the kitchen, and when the twins and their younger brother burst into the room, all eyes turned to see Max, Gil, and Owen hurling themselves like children toward their parents.

The moment she saw them, Emma's eyes filled with tears, and she reached out to pull her sons in close.

"Dad," Max, who had gained an inch or so on his father in the past few months, said with a wide smile as he wrapped his arms around Jonah and squeezed, followed in turn by each of his brothers.

"How long are you here?" Owen asked as he pulled away.

Lucas slipped his arm around his own wife, grateful for the loving display of affection he witnessed. It was not something he'd been privy to as a child, but had, in turn, provided to his daughter—luckily, the same could be said for his brothers' families as well.

August, the youngest of Jonah's boys, came through the back door and as soon as he saw his brothers, he joined the happy reunion. Lucas did not miss the tears that filled the boy's eyes and imagined how much he must have missed them—being the only child left at home and so far away.

"We bought the MacPherson place," August boasted with excitement, and everyone laughed at the repeated announcement, inciting another round of hugs and congratulations.

The sound of the kitchen door opening and closing again, followed by heavy footfalls clomping on the wooden floor, drew everyone's attention to the hallway where Gabe entered the room.

Everyone froze.

CHAPTER SIX

Gabe watched his grandsons beeline it toward the house and figured that now would be as good a time as any to face his fears. The familiar scent of a coming storm stopped him long enough that he looked out over the horizon half expecting to see thick white sheets of evidence.

Christmas was only a few days away. The ground already glittered with snow, but a new storm was coming. His old bones creaked with experience. He strode into the kitchen and through the house, his heavy work boots clomping against the hard, wooden floors. He took a deep breath, then stepped into the large living space at the front of the house where the whole of his little family had gathered. Silence fell across the room, and everyone turned to look at him.

He leaned against the doorway, hands in pockets, and ventured a nod in greeting.

"Don't stop on my account."

Jonah cleared his throat and stepped forward. "Dad," he said with an extended arm.

"Son," Gabe said solemnly, taking his proffered hand.

There was so much he wanted to say, so much that had been left unsaid, but he didn't know how to start. Besides, there was a time and a place, and here, in front of their entire family, was not it.

"I hear congratulations are in order." Gabe noted the awkward strain in his own voice and chastised himself for allowing things to have gone this far.

"Thank you, sir." Jonah nodded, but the contrived smile on his son's face pierced Gabe's brave façade with ease.

"Well, I've got some work to do." He turned and started for

the back door, but called back over his shoulder, "I'm glad you made it safe."

Coward.

As he walked outside, a light flurry of snow drifted past his face, and he looked up into the heavens to see the scattered flakes floating on the darkening sky. He stopped and took another deep breath.

The coming storm wouldn't hold off for long.

He pulled the collar of the wool-lined jacket he wore up around his neck, rubbed his hands together, and determined now would be a good time to light a fire in the potbellied stove he'd dragged into the barn for heat while he worked. It was going to be a long night.

There were still a few of his failed designs in a pile behind the building he could chop up and use for kindling, so he reached inside the door, pulled the ax off the wall, and headed around back.

It didn't take long for him to get into the rhythm of chopping and soon he had quite a nice pile of wood.

"Dad, I…"

Gabe turned back to see Jonah, a stricken look on his face as his gaze flitted between him, the ax, and the pile of broken wood toys and carvings.

"This is just like you," Jonah said. "You may have everyone around here fooled, but I see through your little act." He took a step toward his father and reached down to retrieve what was left of Gabe's first attempt at a dollhouse for Sophia. "Did you ever think that Christmas was something to be celebrated? To be enjoyed? No, I suppose you haven't." He turned to walk away, then stopped as if to say more.

"Jonah, I think you've mis—"

"You know, Dad, I was hoping that moving back here to be around your brothers, to be with Lucas and his family, would have made you a better man, but I see now that it has just made you a better liar." Jonah tossed the remaining piece of the dollhouse roof into Gabe's pile.

"Jonah," Gabe called after him, but his son didn't look back as he stormed away.

Gabe dropped his head and tightened his fists. "Aaaaaah!" he screamed loudly as he swung the ax hard down onto the stump of wood he'd been using. He regretted the action as a twinge of pain shot up his back, and he took a deep breath to ease the spasm.

It was going to take time, but he was determined to show his sons that he was working at being a better man. Prove to them that he recognized his weaknesses, and that he was sorry for everything he'd put them through over the years. For now, he needed to concentrate on what he could control.

Father Christmas.

He couldn't let Mrs. Fawcett or his daughters-in law down. The town. Mr. Collins. Sophia.

Snow now fell in thin sheets outside as he bent with some effort to retrieve the scraps of wood for his fire. It would be good for him to do something productive with his hands. He added the finishing touches to a train, tied the thick woolen string to a bilbo catcher, sanded a set of blocks, and finished carving the last of several wooden animals that belonged to the barn he'd crafted for the youngest Collins boy.

He picked up a small block of wood, hoping to make another spinning top and whistle for some of the other children in town, although he knew the latter was simply a distraction for the real work he needed to finish tonight.

For months he had been working on the newest figure he would add to the nativity in town tomorrow evening, but he hadn't been able to get the face quite right. It had to be special.

It was the face of God.

A chill washed over him, and knowing the hour was late, Gabe set the small wood block he held down on the floor next to the stove and before long had a hot fire burning in its belly. He rubbed his hands together and, with great care, pulled the wooden statue of Mary, Joseph, and the baby Jesus from beneath his worktable and heaved it up onto the countertop.

He stood back a moment to evaluate the work he had done so far. Pleased, he pleaded for further inspiration. After a few minutes of staring at the wood, an idea came to him, and he picked up his chisel and started back to his task.

CHAPTER SEVEN

"I cannot believe the nerve of that man. Chopping up children's toys. As if his ill humor wasn't enough, how could he ruin Christmas for the little ones? Again?" Jonah moved to the window in his room and stared out at the falling snow.

As a child, he had longed for holidays that were spent in merriment with family and close friends. While the traditions of Christmas had still been in their infancy, he'd watched as others enjoyed molding and refining holiday customs with their own families. He'd seen how the season had brought fathers and sons closer and had yearned for some sign that their father still loved them. Wanted them.

Emma walked up behind him and slid her arms beneath his and around his torso.

"Your father is a good man, Jonah," she said firmly before placing a sweet kiss on the back of his shoulder.

He snorted.

The man had everyone fooled—including his wife. He placed a hand over hers and squeezed.

"You always believe the best in others," he said, twisting in her arms to face her. "That," he said kissing her forehead, "is one of the reasons I fell in love with you."

She looked up at him, her eyes knowing and kind. "There is an explanation for what you saw, my love."

"I don't think y—"

"Shhh," Emma said, placing a finger over his lips.

"Have you heard of Father Christmas?"

"You mean, Santa Claus? Jolly Old St. Nick?"

"Not exactly. I mean this little town of Thistleberry has been graced with its very own Father Christmas."

"Okay," he said, scrunching his brows together.

"This Father Christmas has given hope to people all over the town for the past few years. Some families have had food show up on their porches. One couple had been sleeping on the cold floor next to their three children with nary a blanket to keep them warm, and one December afternoon, when they got home from church, they found a large bedframe, mattress, and piles of woolen bedding lying up against their front door."

Jonah opened his mouth to say something, but Emma stopped him.

"Several of the families in Thistleberry are struggling to put food on their tables, yet last year, every child in this town woke up to a toy with his or her name on it and a treat to share with their families."

"So," Jonah said dismissively, "the town has a do-gooder who is helping out their neighbors. That's a nice sentiment, but I don't know what any of this has to do with my father."

"Did you see the nativity in the middle of Town Square as we drove through?"

"The one without a Mary, Joseph, or a baby Jesus?" he asked with a scoff.

"The very one," she said with a smile. "That nativity has served as a beacon of light for the people here who are struggling to make ends meet. Every week during December, a new wooden statue is placed somewhere in the nativity and the townsfolks look forward to the new additions with anticipation and excitement."

"I still don't see what my father has to do with it."

Emma smiled, waiting. She raised her brows.

It took a moment.

"No!" he said disbelievingly.

Emma nodded.

"Your father is trying. Lucy told me that the first few years were a little strained, but after Sophia was born everything changed." Emma slid out of his arms and sat down in one of the chairs at the foot of the bed.

Jonah took the seat opposite her. He leaned down, his elbows on his knees, and rested his forehead in his hands. It just wasn't possible. His father, Gabe Deardon, was doing something nice for others. In secret.

Impossible.

"How do you know all of this? We've been here less than a day."

"Lucy and I have been corresponding for years. She discovered his secret last year when she happened to stumble across some of his carvings out in his shop in the barn."

"And you didn't tell me?"

"Would you have believed me?"

Jonah shook his head. "Probably not."

Then, it hit him.

The sleigh.

Things were beginning to make sense and the pieces were falling into place.

"Your father wants to make up for the mistakes he's made, Jonah. And you, my love, need to let him."

"I'll talk to him in the morning." Jonah felt awful for the things he'd said to his father. He'd been so blinded by the hurts of his past that he hadn't been open to even the possibility that the man could, or would want to change.

Emma patted him on the knee as she stood up. She kissed him lightly.

"That is one of the reasons I love you," she said as she folded back the covers on the bed. "You do what's right. Thank you. You're a great example for our sons. They have turned into good, hard-working, respectable men. Just like their father."

Hard-headed, unforgiving, and blind. She'd forgotten to mention some of his lesser qualities, and he hoped their sons learn from his mistakes and not repeat them. He breathed a chuckle and prayed for the strength to do what was right.

Please, God, be with us all.

CHAPTER EIGHT

Christmas Eve

"Lucy, have you seen my father?" Jonah asked the woman rolling mounds of dough and placing them on a giant baking sheet. His mouth watered at the sweet aroma swirling about the air in the kitchen.

He'd intended to speak with his father that morning, but his Uncle Hank had coaxed him and his boys into competing with some of the cousins at a Christmas festival in town and it had taken the majority of the day. He'd already been out to the barn and had stopped by Gabe's room, but the man seemed to have disappeared.

"You just missed him," Lucy said with a shrug of her shoulders and a conspiratorial smile.

"Missed him?"

She nodded.

"Every year—for the past few anyway, he heads to his cabin up in the hills, just behind the property, on Christmas Eve and returns first thing Christmas morning. He says he needs a few hours to himself, away from the huge crowd that gathers here at Whisper Ridge during the holidays." She winked at him. "Is it still snowing outside?"

"'Fraid so. Doesn't look like it will be letting up anytime soon."

Lucy shook her head. "We haven't seen a storm like this at Christmas for quite some time and I worry that—" she looked at Jonah with squinted eyes and a raised brow.

"Emma told me last night."

"Oh, good. I worry about him being out there alone at his age. His bones are getting a little creaky lately and he's taken more hot baths in the last month than the entire time I've known him." She laughed nervously, then wiped her hands on her apron and walked to the edge of the kitchen.

Jonah had never thought about his father getting old. He had always been so spry and stubborn.

Still stubborn, he thought.

"Sophia," she called, peeking around the wall and up the stairs. "Where is that child? She is supposed to help put the sugar on top of these pies."

"Hello, wife."

Jonah glanced over his shoulder to see Lucas coming into the kitchen, a grin on his face and his hands behind his back.

"Hello, husband," Lucy said, eying Lucas warily. "What are you up to?"

"Nothing…much," he said, leaning over and stealing a kiss.

He brought a small package out from behind him and held in front of her to see.

"What is this?" she asked him, one brow raised.

"I guess you'll have to wait until your hands are clean to open it and find out."

She reached out to grab it from him, but he pulled it away.

"Not with dough all over your hands."

She held up her hands, only slightly covered in flour dust. She tilted her head and smiled coyly.

"Oh, all right," Lucas relented with a mischievous smirk.

He pulled back the twine and unrolled the thick parchment paper so only he could see. His eyes opened wide, and a huge smile spread across his face as he concealed the contents from his wife.

"What? What is it?"

Lucas winked at Jonah, the sly grin still plastered against his face.

Lucy made another grab for it, but she was no match for his brother's height.

"Lucas Deardon!"

His little brother laughed and dropped his hands, turning the parchment around and displaying her surprise in front of her.

"Music!" she exclaimed.

"Eight Christmas tunes to be exact," Lucas said proudly.

Lucy squealed and jumped up into Lucas's arms, wrapping her flour covered hands around his neck and kissing his face.

It was Jonah's turn to laugh as white streaks and prints from Lucy's fingertips smeared his brother's person. It was good to see that his brother had found the same kind of happiness he had with Emma.

Lucas handed Jonah the sheets of music and wrapped his arms around his wife. "I should get you music more often."

She giggled.

"Yes, please."

Jonah looked down at the contents in his hands, genuinely surprised. He couldn't imagine how Gabe would react to such a gift. He turned for the door, feeling as if intruding on their moment, and set the music down on the table where it was out of harm's way.

"Will you go get your daughter?" Jonah heard Lucy say to her husband from behind him.

"If you save me one of those butter-laden bits of heaven for later," Lucas retorted as he joined Jonah in the hallway.

"Let me just go grab Sophia and then we can catch up," he said as he climbed the stairs, taking two at a time. "There is much to be done tonight," he called down, in an obviously jovial mood.

For the first time since being here, Jonah noticed the piano sitting up against the wall just out of the hallway. He looked around, but everyone seemed to be off, busy with one activity or another. He moved closer to the instrument, reaching out and daring to plunk one of the keys. Then another.

Back in Oregon, Emma had sung to her children, but he had not had a piano in his house since the day he watched his father destroy their mother's. He tapped on another key and smiled as the rich, low note reverberated against the air.

Lucas ran down the stairs and back into the kitchen, a look of sheer panic on his face.

Jonah followed, a sinking feeling churning in his belly.

"Sophia's gone," Lucas said, his breathing heavy and ragged. "I've looked everywhere."

"Oh, she's probably just hiding or playing with the other children." Lucy put on a strong face, but the worry in her voice was hard to mask. "Sophia," she called, moving from one room in the large house to the next to no avail.

"I'll go get the others," Jonah told Lucas. He and Noah could gather their uncles and cousins who lived here at Whisper Ridge to help, while Emma, Kate, and the boys could search through the yard and close outbuildings.

Lucas nodded.

"I'm coming with you." He strode to the door, picked up his jacket from the hook there and shoved his arms through the sleeves.

Lucy wrung her hands against her apron. "I'm coming too."

"Someone needs to be here in case she comes back."

"But—" Even as she started, he could see that she knew Lucas made sense, and she dropped her shoulders in resignation.

"Go," she said quietly.

"Lucy," Jonah tried to offer some comfort, "we'll find her."

"Go!" she commanded, and he did not hesitate to obey her order.

With the storm evolving dangerously into a blizzard, there was little time to waste.

CHAPTER NINE

Gabe looked out across the landscape, barely able to make out the markers that offered a sense of direction. The storm had grown increasingly fierce, and he shivered, despite the warmth of Ethel's wool-lined cloak. He pulled the hood up and over his Stetson, grateful it fit, but sure it must look a sight.

As he pulled up near the farmhouse on the farthest edge of Thistleberry, he was careful not to get too close. The last thing he needed was to get caught. Again. He'd mapped out his route early on and had decided to start at the farthest point from Whisper Ridge and work his way back home. That way, he would have no need to backtrack and be more likely to avoid detection.

Each year, it had been his privilege to select three or four families in the area to help. While every child in Thistleberry would receive a toy, these families would receive a little more. It was the least he could do to show his gratitude for everything with which he and his family had been blessed.

Somewhere along the road, he'd forgotten the lessons that his own mother had taught him as a child, but not anymore. He loved hearing about the experiences and excitement that his small acts of kindness brought to others. It was a feeling he'd gone many years without.

If only he could have explained himself to Jonah, shared with his son the joy he'd found in serving others, shared how he hoped to make a difference in even a single life around him. He'd meant to speak with him at breakfast, but he'd worked all through the night, and by the time he had dragged his aching body out of his bed this morning, everyone had already left for the Christmas festival in town, and he'd missed the opportunity.

Gabe hopped down off the sleigh and wrapped the reins around the metal cleat just below the seat on the driver's side. He unhooked the lantern from its post and carried it with him to the back of the sleigh, setting it down on the runner so his hands would be free to retrieve the gifts.

The wind whipped at his face and hands. And the storm didn't show any signs of stopping, so he would need to hurry.

He lifted the lid for the storage compartment at the back only to discover the face of his little Sophia peeking out from beneath a large bundle of fur skins and blankets, sleeping peacefully next to the baby Jesus.

His heart sped up a beat or two.

"Sophia," he called quietly, glancing around to make sure no one was there to see him. He reached down into the compartment and pulled the little girl up into his arms.

She stirred and snuggled into him, then her eyes popped open, and she sat bolt upright.

"I knew it was you, Granddad. *You* are Father Christmas."

"Shhh," Gabe coaxed. While the town seemed empty, several homes had been built around the outskirts and he didn't want to risk exposure. "Sophia, you darling girl," he hugged her close, "your parents are going to be worried sick."

"Don't worry, Granddad. I left them a note."

"Since when do you know how to write a note?"

"Mama is teaching me. She says it will be better when I start school if I already know how to write my letters and numbers," she responded proudly. "I like your coat."

Gabe tapped the tip of her nose and chuckled softly. He doubted the child could write a note clearly enough that Lucas would understand where she'd gone. It was all the more reason to hurry. He set her down on the back seat, pulled out the furs and woolen blankets from the back, and wrapped her warmly inside of them so only a small portion of her face could be seen.

"Stay," he warned, but couldn't help the smile that reached his face. "And we need to be very quiet, Sophia. Can you do that for me?"

In barely more than a whisper she responded, "Yes, sir."

With a satisfied nod, Gabe strode to the back of the sleigh and scooped up the large potato sack in which he'd placed all this family's gifts, slung it up and over his shoulder, then started for the front door.

A shadow alerted him that someone approached, and he ducked out of sight. The lady of the house passed by the window, glancing out through the curtains at the snow, then closed them up tight. Gabe waited just long enough that he thought it would be safe, then started again for the door.

Slowly, he lifted the sack from his shoulders and set it up onto the covered porch, leaning it against the house where it would be safer from the elements until it could be discovered, then he quietly tromped through the snow as he made his way back to the sleigh and to his granddaughter.

He blew out a long breath. One down several more to go.

"Are you doing all right, little one?" he asked as he climbed back up onto the driver's seat and returned the lantern to its post.

She nodded. "This is fun."

"Well, I'm glad you think so. And remember, you cannot tell anyone about this."

"Not even mama?"

Gabe chuckled.

"Your mama already knows."

"Of course, she does. My mama knows everything."

All of the remaining stops lay on route back to Whisper Ridge. He slapped the reins, heading as quickly as he dared toward town. He glanced back over his shoulder to see his granddaughter's cherubic face visible in the humble lantern's light. Her rosy cheeks had been scrunched into little balls just beneath her eyes as she smiled up at him.

At least the child appeared warm.

As they rode, the sound of Sophia's little angelic voice humming, then singing carols of Christmas, enveloped Gabe with warmth. He'd forgotten how sweet music could be and reveled in this special moment with his granddaughter.

Each time they stopped at someone's home, Sophia would go silent as the delivery was made. They repeated the action several times before reaching town.

The streets were quiet, the only light coming from the hotel at the far end of the boardwalk. All of the businesses in Thistleberry had shut down early today after the Christmas festival so folks could go home and be with their families.

He guided the horses slowly into the middle of Town Square and climbed down off the sleigh. His bones creaked and his body was stiff, but he reminded himself again that it was for a good cause.

Gabe again walked around to the back of the sleigh and reached in to retrieve the heavy wooden statue. Even with all the other pieces he had placed there over the years, the nativity had seemed empty to him until the moment he set the beautiful figure of Mary holding the Christ-child and Joseph kneeling behind them down in the once vacant center.

It was complete.

The piece had turned out much better than he could have ever expected, and he took a moment to admire the scene. He smiled as his focus fell on the babe. This reminder of the reason they celebrated Christmas was his gift to Thistleberry this year.

I hope you like it.

Voices came from down the covered walkway around the corner from them. With the snow coming down even faster now, Gabe hustled to the sleigh and, with just a light tap of the reins, the horses seemed to know exactly what to do as they headed down to the opposite end of the street and across the bridge to the road that would take them home.

Just one more stop. The Collins farmhouse was the last on the list and sat just south of Raine's place.

This house was a little trickier to get to without calling any attention to oneself. There was a large picket fence that surrounded the home and past experience had told him that the gate squeaked. He pulled out the oil can he'd tucked under the seat and made quick work of greasing the hinge, then grabbed ahold of the gate and gingerly pulled it toward him.

No squeak.

With relief, he set the oil back into the sleigh.

The Collins family consisted of seven children ranging in ages from three to fifteen and their parents. Gabe had handcrafted simple toys for each of the younger children, and more complex games and puzzles for the older ones, along with some foodstuffs, a little money, and a small jewelry box for their mother. He'd also put together a collection of woodworking tools for Mr. Collins.

As he set the last two bags on their porch, he smiled to himself, wishing he could see their faces in the morning. He shook his head at the thought, then made his way down the steps, out the gate, and toward his granddaughter. He needed to get the girl home.

He lost his footing on a small patch of ice just as he approached the sleigh and fell backward, knocking his head against the hard ground and twisting his knee.

"Granddad?"

Gabe heard Sophia's faint cry as darkness threatened to overtake him. He fought the blackness. Couldn't relent. He had to keep her safe. When the little girl reached him, she held up the lantern that, by some miracle, had not broken in the fall. He tried to focus on her face. Then, watched as her forehead crinkled, her eyes glazed over with tears, and her lips shook—whether from the cold or with fear he was unsure.

"Granddad," she called again, "are you all right?" she asked innocently.

Gabe fought to sit up, but his head swirled, and his leg throbbed. He just needed a minute, and he lay back against the snow, the thick wool-lined cloak Ethel had provided for his adventures the only barrier between him and the cold.

"Soph," he called up to the child, "don't you worry none. Everything is going to be okay," he tried to offer as much comfort as he could.

His little angel set down the lantern and crawled inside of his coat, snuggling up to his chest.

All he could do was to put his arm around her, hoping that the warmth of his cloak would protect her from the unrelenting snow, and he pulled her close as he worked to catch his breath.

CHAPTER TEN

Two hours had passed and there was still no sign of Sophia.

Uncle Hank and Uncle Sam, along with their families, had all come over to join in the search. The women and children had stayed closer to the homestead—searching the outbuildings and surrounding landmarks, and some of them had stayed behind with Lucy in the ranch house to keep her from going mad with worry.

Where could she have gone?

The weather was bad enough that the men had chosen to go out in pairs. The last thing they needed was to lose someone else. Jonah and Noah had travelled south toward Raine's place, while Lucas and their cousin, Seth, had gone north toward Happenstance and the MacPherson place. They had agreed to return to the ranch to regroup and to check in every hour.

Jonah looked at the men who had gathered back around the corral. Solemn shakes of their heads indicated that Sophia had not yet been found. The sound of the rushing creek hit Jonah like a punch to the gut, but he refused to believe she would have ventured that far. Besides, his cousin, Daniel, and Uncle Sam had already checked that direction and had come back empty-handed—to everyone's relief.

Raine pulled up on his horse and dismounted next to him.

"Sheriff," Jonah said, pulling his cousin into a hug.

"Any luck?"

"Not yet."

Lucas and Noah also pulled the man into a hug.

"Thanks for coming, Raine. I can't imagine she got far in this weather." They spent the next couple of minutes catching him up on where everyone had already gone looking for little Sophia.

"Well, if she is half as smart as her mama, which I know her to be, she is probably cuddled up somewhere, toasty warm, without a care in the world." Raine mounted his horse. "A lot of folks, especially those on the smaller farms, will have their animals sheltered up to avoid the storm. She may have hunkered down in someone's barn."

No matter where she'd gone, a little girl wouldn't last long if she remained out in this storm, alone. Jonah could only imagine how scared she must be, but they had to keep hope.

"You three want to come with me?" Raine asked.

"All right, everybody. I know you're cold and tired and worried about our little Sophia. She's a smart little girl and will likely have taken shelter somewhere if she couldn't find her way back home."

Jonah and his brothers all mounted their horses.

"Lucas!" Lucy ran out into the yard just in time to catch them before they'd headed back out.

Her husband jumped down off his mare and ran toward her.

"I found this in Sophia's room." She handed her husband a small piece of paper.

After studying it for a moment with scrunched brows, Lucas handed it up to Jonah.

It was a drawing of his father's new sleigh with stick-like images of toys sticking out of the back.

"You don't think she…?" Lucy's question trailed.

"Yes," Lucas said with confidence. "I definitely think she would. She loves that man and was fascinated by the sleigh. She thinks he's Father Christmas and it's Christmas Eve."

Lucy raised her brows.

"Do you know where he was headed?" Noah asked.

Lucy nodded, then proceeded to tell them the names of the different families Gabe had chosen to help this year.

"But, he would have also stopped by the center of town," she added, "to place the new piece in the nativity."

Lucas kissed his wife.

"We'll find them," he said, then mounted his horse, following the men down the dark and snowy road.

"The Collins place is closest," Lucas informed them, yelling to be heard over the sound of the wind as it blew large snowflakes in several directions at once. "We'll start there."

As they approached a small farmhouse, Jonah caught a glimpse of light coming from the snow, and the muffled sound of anxious horses swirled in the air.

"Over there!" he yelled to his brothers as he pointed in the direction of the house ahead.

With a quick slap of his reins, he approached the light and discovered his father's sleigh, but there was no sign of him or the little girl.

"Dad!" Noah yelled as he jumped down off his horse and ran toward a snow-covered lump just outside the Collins' front gate.

In moments, Lucas, Jonah, and Raine joined them. Jonah held his breath as Noah leaned down, placing his ear against their father's face to check for breath.

"Come on, Dad," Jonah said aloud.

His heart nearly jumped from his chest as his father's eyes opened and he began struggling to get up.

"Dad, where's Sophia?" Lucas asked in desperation.

Gabe opened his jacket to reveal the little girl cuddling up against him. One look at Lucas and she pushed away from her grandfather and jumped up, no worse for the wear.

"Daddy!" she squealed raising her hands to him.

Jonah's heart swelled with warmth as Lucas swept Sophia up in his arms and spun her around in circles, holding her close against him. He buried his face in her curls, his body shaking with emotion, then pulled back, kissing her face, her cheeks, her head.

She was all right.

As Jonah reached down on one side and Noah on the other to help their father to his feet, he said a silent prayer of gratitude.

They were both all right.

"What happened, Dad?" Noah asked. "We've been looking for Sophia for hours."

Gabe wobbled one direction, then another and his arms shot out to steady himself against his sons.

"She stowed away in the back with all the blankets and toys." He tried to take a step, but his knee buckled beneath him, and he groaned in pain.

"Blasted leg," he grumped.

Jonah positioned himself under his father's arm and Noah did the same on the other side and they heaved him toward the sleigh.

"Am I in trouble, Daddy?" Sophia asked as they got closer.

Lucas laughed through his tears. "No, baby. But never ever leave again without talking to me or Mama first, all right?"

"But, Daddy,…" she said with a hint of protest.

Lucas looked at her with a raised brow.

"Yes, sir," she said quickly before she leaned in close to him. "Granddad is Father Christmas," she whispered, then placed a finger over her lips. "Isn't that wonderful?"

Everyone laughed.

She was safe. They were all safe.

CHAPTER ELEVEN

Christmas Day

Jonah had never seen so many of his relatives in one place at the same time. Laughter rang through the room like a welcome guest spreading its Christmas joy. The savory aromas of roasted meats and salted potatoes mingled with the sweet scent of several confectionary delicacies.

He looked over at Emma, who beamed at her boys as they recounted their adventures since coming to Whisper Ridge and Jonah smiled. Moving here had been the right decision.

The afternoon promised a good time with a plethora of Deardon family traditions and festivities—many he had never even heard of.

"Dad," Jonah said, shifting in his seat to look at his father. "I just want to tell you—"

"We both made mistakes, son," Gabe said, patting him on the shoulder. "Let's leave it at that. It's time we look forward and work at being a family again." He winked. "And now that you're moving into the MacPherson place, well, we'll have plenty of time to catch up." His father clapped him on the back. "What do you say we have some of that pie?"

Relief washed over Jonah like a warm bath. He'd finally found peace.

"I have to admit, I'm a little jealous that you all will be living so close to each other. I hate to leave knowing everyone else will be here," Noah said as he squeezed his wife's hand.

"Do you think any more of your neighbors will be selling?" Kate chimed in.

"Tarnation," Gabe said without hesitation, "we'll build you a place."

Everyone laughed.

"I think it's time we hear our Lucy play something on the piano," Uncle Hank called from the other end of the table.

Lucy wiped the corner of her mouth with her napkin and jumped up. She grabbed the music Lucas had given her from the armoire in the corner and sat down to play.

Silent Night.

Jonah looked at his father and shifted uneasily in his seat. Music had not been allowed in their home since their mother had left more than thirty years ago and he feared his father's reaction to the carol. The peace he'd felt just moments ago was suddenly stripped from him and he held his breath as the verse began.

"Silent night. Holy night. All is calm…" everyone sang.

Then it happened. Something Jonah could have never expected.

"All is bright." The small sound coming from his father grew. "Round yon virgin, mother and child. Holy infant so tender and mild."

Everyone else had stopped singing, but Gabe just sang louder.

"Sleep in heavenly peace." His gravelly voice quieted to almost a whisper. "Sleep in heavenly peace."

Jonah wiped the tear that streamed down his face and started in on the second verse with the rest of his family.

He was home.

Reviews for AN ANGEL IN THISTLEBERRY are both welcomed and appreciated. They can be as short or as long as you'd like. Even a star rating is wonderful and valued. Thanks tons!

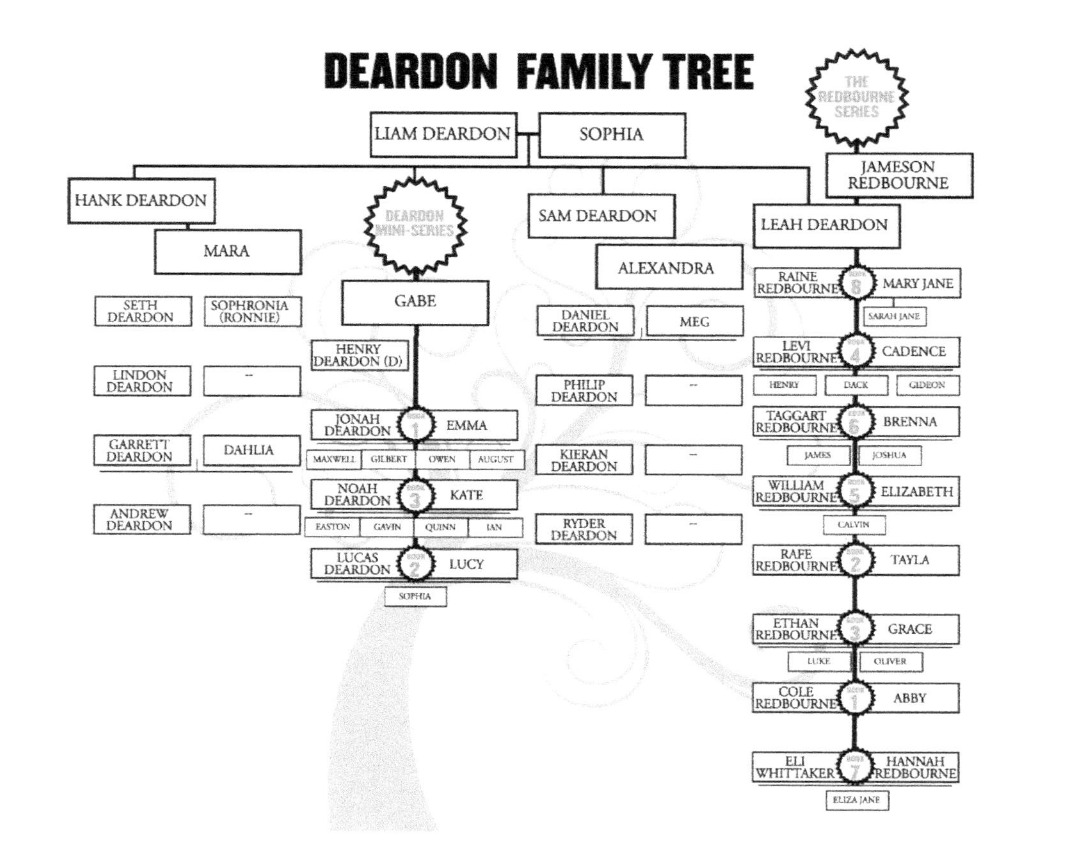
DEARDON FAMILY TREE
THE REDBOURNE SERIES
LIAM DEARDON
SOPHIA
HANK DEARDON
MARA
SETH DEARDON
SOPHRONIA (RONNIE)
LINDON DEARDON
--
GARRETT DEARDON
DAHLIA
ANDREW DEARDON
--
DEARDON MINI-SERIES
GABE
HENRY DEARDON (D)
JONAH DEARDON
1
EMMA
MAXWELL
GILBERT
OWEN
AUGUST
NOAH DEARDON
3
KATE
EASTON
GAVIN
QUINN
IAN
LUCAS DEARDON
2
LUCY
SOPHIA
SAM DEARDON
ALEXANDRA
DANIEL DEARDON
MEG
PHILIP DEARDON
--
KIERAN DEARDON
--
RYDER DEARDON
--
JAMESON REDBOURNE
LEAH DEARDON
RAINE REDBOURNE
8
MARY JANE
SARAH JANE
LEVI REDBOURNE
4
CADENCE
HENRY
DACK
GIDEON
TAGGART REDBOURNE
6
BRENNA
JAMES
JOSHUA
WILLIAM REDBOURNE
5
ELIZABETH
CALVIN
RAFE REDBOURNE
2
TAYLA
ETHAN REDBOURNE
3
GRACE
LUKE
OLIVER
COLE REDBOURNE
1
ABBY
ELI WHITTAKER
7
HANNAH REDBOURNE
ELIZA JANE

ABOUT THE AUTHOR

KELLI ANN MORGAN is the international bestselling author of the beloved Redbourne Series, Deardon Mini-Series, and the Silver Springs Series. She writes inspirational romances with handsome, chivalrous men, strong, intelligent women, and a host of other characters that will feel like family. Her novels are highly romantic, full of action, and always leave you with a happily-ever-after. She lives in northern Utah near the beautiful mountains where she writes, runs her graphic design business, and enjoys many creative and artistic hobbies.

You can learn more about Kelli Ann and her books by visiting her website at www.kelliannmorgan.com or visit her on Facebook. If you would like to receive new release alerts, bonus content, and more, please sign up for her newsletter.

FACEBOOK:
https://www.facebook.com/KelliAnnMorganAuthor

E-MAIL:
kelliann@kelliannmorgan.com

NEWSLETTER SIGN UP:
https://bit.ly/2LPdgYY

Printed in Great Britain
by Amazon